The Always-Late Angel

by Diane Stortz

Illustrated by Joe Stites

Once there was a little angel who was always late for choir practice.

When she should have been singing with the heavenly choir, she was usually out gathering sunbeams,

riding on a comet, or swinging on a star.

That's where she was when Gabriel told the angel choir that baby Jesus would soon be born on earth.

"We are all going to earth to sing the good news!" said Gabriel. Every angel was excited, and off they all flew.

When the little angel remembered that she was supposed to be at choir practice, she hurried back to heaven. But she was too late. She couldn't hear any singing. "Where are all the angels in the angel choir?" she asked the gatekeeper.

"Why, they've gone to earth to sing the good news that baby Jesus has been born," said the gatekeeper.

"Oh, my goodness!" said the little angel. "I'd better try to catch up with them!"

But she was too late. The angel choir had already sung their heavenly songs and gone back to heaven. All the little angel could see were some sleepy sheep.

"I wonder where I should go now," said the little angel. "Baaaa," said a sheep. "To Bethlehem!" said the little angel, and she hurried toward the little town.

In the quiet streets of Bethlehem the little angel saw some shepherds. They were talking about a baby they had seen in a stable!

The little angel flew over Bethlehem, looking for the stable. "I see it!" she said. Inside the stable were Mary and Joseph and baby Jesus.

The little angel tiptoed to the baby's bed. Baby Jesus looked up at her and smiled. Then the little angel sang him a heavenly song. She hadn't been late for Christmas after all!